ZARTOG'S
REMOTE

ZARTOG'S
REMOTE

Herbie Brennan
and Neal Layton

BLOOMSBURY
CHILDREN'S
BOOKS

First published in Great Britain in 2000
Bloomsbury Publishing Plc, 38 Soho Square, London, W1D 3HB

Copyright © Text Herbie Brennan 2000
Copyright © Illustrations Neal Layton 2000

The moral right of the author has been asserted
A CIP catalogue record of this book is available from the
British Library

ISBN 0 7475 5185 5

Printed in Great Britain by Clays Ltd, St Ives plc

10 9 8 7 6 5 4 3 2 1

For Sarah Hutchinson and Donna Marks, to keep a promise – H.B.

For Eric, Peach, Joshua and all my furry friends – N.L.

One

Zartog was a little person with several arms, enormous eyes and nearly no nose whatsoever.

The reason he had nearly no nose was that he didn't smell.

The enormous eyes were for night vision. He could read a newspaper at fifty yards in the bottom of a coal mine after midnight.

He had several arms because he came from a planet circling round the star Sirius in the constellation of Orion.

He was little because he was only eight years old.

But Zartog was very advanced for his age. That's why all three of his parents agreed to let him drive a flying saucer.

'Don't exceed the speed limit,' warned his mother.

'I won't, Mater,' promised Zartog.

'Don't go any further than Orion's Belt,' said his father.

'I won't, Pater,' promised Zartog.

'And above all, don't touch the warp drive,' growled his grather.

'I won't, Gater,' promised Zartog.

He closed the door of his glistening metallic craft and strapped himself into

the pilot's seat. He picked up the remote control and pointed it at the computer.

'Take off,' he instructed.

'Like, wow, right away, man,' the computer said.

There was a small vibration as the saucer took off straight up. Zartog's three parents waved fondly after it.

Zartog waved back briefly then turned to the computer.

'Ignore all speed limits,' he instructed.

'Like, wow, wicked!' the computer exclaimed.

The engine note climbed into ultrasonic as the craft ripped up towards the speed of light.

'Head beyond Orion's Belt,' Zartog instructed.

'Like, wow, far out!' cried the computer.

The saucer took a bearing on the twin suns of Sirius, then headed like an arrow for the depths of Outer Space.

Zartog took a deep breath. 'Engage warp drive,' he instructed.

'Like, wow, cool!' the computer sighed ecstatically.

The warp drive cut in.

It was a BIG mistake.

Two

Rachel was a little person with enormous eyes and hair that stuck out as if she'd plugged her nose into an electric socket.

The reason for the frizzy hair was that she'd had an Afro styling on her birthday.

She had enormous eyes because of her poor vision. She wore great round gold-rimmed glasses that made them appear huge.

She was little because, like Zartog, she was only eight years old. Her years were a different length from his, of course, as were her ears, although that hadn't much to do with anything.

Rachel didn't come from a planet circling Sirius in the constellation of

Orion. She came from a planet circling
Sol in the Milky Way. It was a strange
planet where noses run and feet smell.

Some weird life forms had evolved on
this planet. Three of them were called
Sammy Tucks, Tom Barlow and Elvis
Fine.

Sammy, Tom and Elvis were very much
alike, even though they weren't brothers
or even related.

They all had haircuts so close they
looked shaved.

They all wore bovver boots and faded jeans.

None of them ever washed and they all avoided work.

They liked to hang about outside the school to beat up little kids.

Especially little kids who were a different colour from themselves.

Rachel saw them at the street corner and felt instantly afraid. She didn't want to walk past them, but there was no other way for her to go.

'Here comes Frizzhead,' sneered Elvis
Fine.

'Let's duff her up,' suggested Sammy
Tucks.

The three of them began to walk
towards Rachel. They had a peculiar way
of walking, all hip movement and
swagger.

Rachel's insides turned to water, but
she had the good sense not to show it.

'Where do you think you're going,

Frizzhead?' asked Tom Barlow.

'I'm going home,' Rachel said.

'But you're walking on our street,' said Elvis Fine.

'And anybody walks on our street has to pay a fee,' said Sammy Tucks.

They all grinned at her horribly.

'It's not your street, it's everybody's street!' said Rachel bravely. 'And anyway I don't have any money.'

'Then you can't get past,' said Elvis Fine. He stepped directly in front of her.

Rachel kicked him in the knee.

'Yow!' yelled Elvis Fine, hopping on one leg.

Rachel dashed past him and raced down the street.

'I'll get you for that, Frizzhead!' he roared after her. 'I'll get you for that tomorrow!'

The trouble was she knew he would.

And tomorrow she wouldn't be able to take him by surprise.

Three

Lord Percy was a little person with four short legs, one wet nose and a sad expression.

The reason he had four short legs was to keep his tum from scraping on the ground.

The reason he had a wet nose was it smelled thirty thousand times better than the dry noses owned by most two-legged creatures. However, when the rest of him got wet, he smelled thirty thousand times worse than most two-legged creatures.

This was one of life's great mysteries.

The reason he had a sad expression was that his mother had been frightened by a bloodhound. But Lord Percy wasn't sad and never had been.

Lord Percy was just bored.

Rachel, who seemed to understand everything he said, still hadn't come home from school. Rachel's mother was out shopping. Rachel's father was in the bottom field making hay.

Lord Percy had nobody to play with.

He wandered listlessly through the house.

He wandered into the kitchen, but couldn't find a single bone.

He wandered into the three bedrooms and left some hairs on the eiderdowns.

He wandered into the living room.

In the living room he found the black box the grown-ups watched most evenings and decided to give it a go.

The remote control was on the arm of the couch. Lord Percy climbed up, grabbed it and pointed.

Nothing happened.

He tried pointing again.

Still nothing happened.

Thoroughly fed up, Lord Percy carried

the remote through the flap in the back
door, across the meadow and into the
little wood.

He chewed it a bit and tossed it into the
air.

Then he trotted back to the house to
wait for Rachel.

The remote control lay where he left it,
in a clearing in the middle of the wood.

Four

Zartog stared through the window of his flying saucer. Below him was the huge blue and white ball of an alien planet, the third one from a yellow alien sun.

It was absolutely forbidden to land on an alien planet if you were Zartog's age.

It was forbidden by the Grand Council for Forbidden Things.

It was forbidden by the Popess of Religion.

It was forbidden by the Leader of the Purple Clans.

It was forbidden by seventeen historical treaties with the Arks and the Quarks and the Grumbelines.

It was forbidden by all three of Zartog's parents.

Zartog pointed the remote. 'Land saucer,' he instructed.

'Like, wow, heavy!' gasped the computer admiringly.

The saucer plunged into the atmosphere of the alien planet. At once it started to glow.

Radar stations across the globe picked up the trace, but the operators ignored it because they didn't believe in flying saucers.

The saucer flew over Beijing, but the Chinese just thought somebody was juggling plates.

The saucer flew over New York, but the New Yorkers shrugged it off as a publicity stunt.

The saucer flew over Dublin, but the

Irish put it down to Guinness.

In Lapland they thought it must be Santa's reindeer on a practice run.

Chile had turned chilly, so everybody went indoors and missed the saucer altogether.

Easter Island also missed it altogether because the saucer flew across at Pentecost.

The Swedes mistook it for a turnip.

The Japanese decided it was one of their own inventions.

It was siesta time in Spain and nobody woke up.

The saucer flew over London. Nobody noticed because it was four o'clock and they were having tea.

Eventually the saucer hovered over a clearing in a wood located on a farm outside a small town in the Home Counties.

'Like, wow, a suitable landing space has been found,' the computer reported.

Five

Lord Percy bounced out to greet Rachel
as she came home from school.

'Hello, Lord Percy,' Rachel said,
tickling his ears. 'Where's Mummy?'

'Woof,' Lord Percy said.

'Still shopping?' Rachel asked in some
surprise. 'What about Daddy?'

'Woof,' Lord Percy said.

'Not finished the haymaking yet?' Rachel shook her head and tutted. She shrugged off her schoolbag. 'What have you been doing then?'

'Woof, woof, woof!' Lord Percy said.

'Playing in the woods again?' asked Rachel. 'Well, you'd better show me.'

Together they left the house and ran across the meadow.

As they did so, there was a strange musical humming overhead. Beyond the meadow, trees in the little wood began to

whip back and forth, as if driven by a mighty wind.

The humming noise got so loud it made her ears ache.

Lord Percy stopped running, sat down and looked up.

'Woof,' he said.

Rachel looked up too. 'Good grief,' she said, 'I think you're right!'

She watched wide-eyed as an enormous, saucer-shaped aircraft swung low above her head, narrowly missing the tops of the trees.

It hovered for a moment, then made a landing somewhere in the middle of the wood.

The humming stopped. But she could still see a bright light shining through the trees.

She looked and hesitated, hesitated and looked. 'What do you think we should do?' she asked Lord Percy.

'Woof,' Lord Percy said.

Rachel nodded. 'Yes, I think so too.'

Together they ran towards the wood.

Six

Zartog unfastened his seat belt and slipped the remote into his pocket. He sang the note that opened the saucer door and caused a glittering silver ramp to slide out onto the ground.

'Forbidden to breathe alien air,' the computer warned. 'Forbidden to touch alien soil.'

'Like, wow, scary!' Zartog said and walked down the ramp.

He found himself in the middle of a group of great, tall, slow life forms.

Their feet were buried deep in the ground. Their arms reached high into the sky. They had flat, veined, green fingers that ate sunlight and turned it into sugar.

They reminded Zartog of his uncle.

'Take me to your leader,' he demanded.

While he waited for the great slow answer, Zartog walked about a bit.

There were other, faster life forms living in the neighbourhood.

Nut-eating life forms with bushy tails lived in the arms of the great slow life forms.

Blind life forms dug tunnels underneath the great slow life forms.

Tiny flying life forms buzzed and bit and flitted, making a great nuisance of themselves.

A hopping life form with big ears twitched its nose at Zartog from behind a bush.

It hopped into the open and stared at Zartog with a brace of bright and beady eyes.

It hopped across the clearing and began to nibble Zartog's toes.

Zartog read its mind and found it thought he was a lettuce.

'Shoo!' he said, waving several of his arms about.

The hopping life form ignored him.

Since it was pleasant having his toes nibbled, Zartog waited quite some time before he said 'Shoo!' again.

He must have said it louder this time because the hopping life form stopped nibbling and looked up at him.

'Shoo!' said Zartog for a third time. He

changed his colouring from green to
fearsome puce, jumped up and down
four times, then chased the hopping life
form all the way across the clearing.

As he did so, the remote control slipped
from his pocket and fell into a bush.

Seven

As the hopping life form disappeared,
Zartog suddenly heard two new life forms
approaching. He glanced over his
shoulder and all seven of his inner oils
ran cold.

They were both fast life forms. One was

as big as he was and even looked a little like him in an ugly, alien sort of way.

The other was much smaller, but packed full of fierceness, growls and teeth.

They both looked extremely scary, like the mungowarbles on the planet Squat.

'Help!' Zartog murmured. He reached for his remote control to change them into something harmless.

His remote control was gone.

The larger of the two new life forms

wore huge, terrifying lenses on its eyes. Zartog knew these were meant to concentrate its angry glare so that his second stomach would fill up with wobble jelly.

The smaller of the two new life forms said 'Woof!'

Although Zartog hadn't switched on his universal translator, he knew the sound meant 'Stand still, I say, so that my large companion may glare you to death and quite possibly eat you.'

He looked around, hearts pounding. The remote was lying in the middle of the clearing. Zartog ran and snatched it up. It looked as if something had been chewing it.

Zartog stared at the chewed remote in despair. Even though it might not be entirely broken, he could not take the risk.

As the approaching life forms came closer still, he raced for his saucer, ran

three times around it as he had been
taught, then rushed up the ramp.

He sang the emergency song.

The ramp slid up, the main door
slammed shut and the saucer blinked into
a holding orbit seven miles above the
surface of the planet.

Zartog leaned against a bulkhead and
tried to catch his breath.

It had been a very narrow escape.

Eight

Rachel watched in wonder. She was so excited she could hardly stand.

The little person ran three times round the flying saucer, then rushed up the ramp.

Before she could really grasp what was happening, the saucer blinked into the air.

In a moment it had disappeared.

'Woof,' said Lord Percy in surprise.

Rachel ran into the clearing at once.

The grass was beaten down, but otherwise there was no sign that a flying saucer had landed.

Even with Lord Percy as a witness, nobody would believe what she'd just seen.

Desperately she searched for something –
anything – that would prove her story.

Eventually she noticed something
caught up in a bush.

Rachel ran across and fished it out. To
her disappointment, it was just the
remote control for the television set at
home.

She turned it over in her hand,
frowning. How had it got out here into
the middle of a bush?

She turned to Lord Percy and glared at him. 'Have you been playing with the remote control again?' she asked severely.

'Woof,' Lord Percy said, but would not catch her eye.

Rachel dropped the remote control into the pocket of her dress and walked back to the house.

Nine

Zartog climbed into the pilot's seat and pointed his remote control.

'Return to Sirius,' he instructed.

'Like, wrong remote,' said the computer.

Zartog glanced at the remote control. Except for the teeth marks, it looked exactly like the remote he'd been using all along.

Then he turned it over. There was something stamped in tiny letters near the bottom.

Zartog twisted his left ear to activate the universal translator plugged into his brain.

At once the writing became clear. It said made in Hong Kong.

He hurled the remote onto the floor so fiercely that it bounced.

'Like, wow, temper temper,' the computer remarked.

Quite suddenly Zartog felt very small and very lost.

'I want to go home!' he told the computer. 'I want to go home now!'

'Hey, man,' the computer told him kindly, 'I'd like to oblige – I really would.

But you know the score as well as anybody. When you got the right remote, you can do anything you want. But when you ain't, you can't.'

'But I haven't got the right remote!' screamed Zartog angrily. 'I've only got this stupid thing made in Hong Kong!'

'So sue me,' the computer told him. 'I don't make the rules.'

Ten

As Rachel walked into the living room, it occurred to her that she might not have been the only one to see the flying saucer.

For all she knew, it might be on the Six O'Clock News.

She turned on the television and threw herself down on the couch. Lord Percy climbed up and sat approvingly beside her.

The picture popped up in a blare of applause as somebody won a car. Rachel pointed the remote control and pressed the button to change to BBC.

The television set turned into a teddy bear.

'Woof?' Lord Percy blinked.

Rachel's hand jerked in surprise and

she pressed the CHANNEL-CHANGE button again. The teddy bear turned into a vacuum cleaner.

Rachel sat staring at the vacuum cleaner for a moment. Very, very cautiously she pressed the CHANNEL-CHANGE button again.

The vacuum cleaner turned into a plate of egg and chips.

Lord Percy jumped down off the couch and headed for the chips.

Hurriedly Rachel pressed the CHANNEL-CHANGE again. The plate of egg and chips turned into a shepherd's crook.

Press. The crook turned into a lawn mower.

Press. The lawn mower turned into a school bag.

Press. The school bag turned into a sheepskin rug.

Rachel kept pressing and pressing until, eventually, a stamp album turned into the television set again.

With a huge sense of relief, she sank back on the couch and pressed the TURN OFF button so she could think.

The television set disappeared.

Eleven

Zartog looked out of the window and tried to pick his home sun Sirius from all the billion stars that studded the huge depths of space.

'I can't stay here for ever,' he remarked to the computer.

'Hey, like, actually you can,' the computer told him logically. 'Not such a hot idea though.'

'But how can I get home?' wailed Zartog.

'Hey, man, all you need is the right remote!'

It was the same conversation that had been going on for so long Zartog had lost track of time. But it felt like maybe 1.782422 hours.

Eventually, in desperation, Zartog said, 'But how do I get the right remote?'

The computer sighed. 'Man,' it said, 'I thought you'd never ask!'

There was a high-pitched whining sound, 'Emergency computer override!' announced the computer loudly.

Zartog grabbed his seat as the saucer banked sharply left.

'Authorisation Alpha, Beta, Gamma, Delta, 778.98778 Tulip, Tango, Foxtrot!' the computer sang.

Zartog felt his stomachs lurch as the craft looped a moebius loop.

'Stated emergency: one lost remote!' the computer howled.

Zartog's eyes crossed as the saucer straightened then moved off at breakneck speed.

'What's going on?' he asked.

'Like, wow, man, everything is in my power!' the computer told him joyfully.

Twelve

At the exact moment the television set disappeared, Rachel's father walked into the room.

Rachel hurriedly stuffed the remote control behind a cushion. She held her breath as her father collapsed into his favourite easy chair, directly facing where the set had been.

'Blessed sheep got loose again,' he said.

Rachel waited, looking innocent. She noticed Lord Percy was looking innocent as well

'Did you feed the chickens?' her father asked.

'Woof,' said Lord Percy.

Rachel nodded. 'Yes, Dad.'

She waited.

He pushed himself up out of the chair with a sigh. 'Well, no rest for the wicked farmer!' he exclaimed.

He walked right across the space where the television had been and left the room.

'Woof,' said Lord Percy in relief.

Rachel watched the door close in amazement.

With trembling fingers she dug out the remote control and pointed it at the place where the television had been.

She pressed the ON button.

The television set reappeared in a blare of music as the Mighty Morphin' Power Rangers leaped across the screen.

Her father stuck his head around the door. 'I hope you're not wasting time watching television if you've got homework to do?'

'No, Dad,' Rachel said.

She got up and carefully turned the power off at the set.

Thirteen

The saucer whizzed out of orbit and set a course that put the sun at Zartog's back.

It buzzed Mars so Zartog could see the huge Face the Martians carved to advertise face cream.

'Like, commercial,' the computer remarked.

It dodged through the Asteroid Belt that formed when an Asteroider called Bode invented very, very high explosive and blew up his planet.

'Like, tragic,' murmured the computer.

It ripped past Jupiter with the Great Red Spot that marked the place the Grumbelines touched down in the Gold Rush of '98.

'Like, historical,' the computer said.

From Jupiter they flew to Saturn, which was surrounded by a massive ring.

'What's that for?' asked Zartog who hadn't noticed it on the way in.

'Man, that keeps the planet from, you know, falling over,' the computer told him.

'Like, gyroscopic,' Zartog said.

The saucer circled Saturn seven times then slingshot itself at breakneck speed towards Uranus.

'Like, nobody lives there any more,' the computer volunteered.

Zartog stared down at the frozen, barren surface of the planet. It looked a really nice place to live. 'Why not?' he asked.

'Property prices got too high,' the computer told him.

From Uranus they flew to Neptune then to Pluto.

'Know what?' asked the computer.

'What what?' asked Zartog back.

'Earth people think Pluto is, like, this dopey dog that talks.'

Zartog and the computer giggled together at the silliness of the Earth people.

The saucer hurled itself beyond the solar system. Behind Zartog's back, the sun got smaller and smaller until it turned into a twinkling star.

It felt as if they might be going home, but Zartog noticed the computer didn't engage warp drive. That meant it would take maybe forty billion years to get there.

But suddenly the saucer slowed.

'What's happening?' asked Zartog cautiously.

'Look out the window, man,' suggested the computer.

Zartog looked out of the window.

Hanging in the dark depths of space was a gigantic cylinder.

It was bigger than the saucer, bigger than any ship he'd ever seen. So far as he could tell, it was bigger than the country he'd landed in when he lost his remote.

It was spinning very fast indeed.

As he watched, the saucer gently shifted its position so that it was facing the huge cylinder end-on. From this angle, Zartog could see the cylinder was surrounded by rings of glowing light.

One ring was glowing violet.

One ring was glowing red.

One ring was glowing white.

One ring was glowing black, which was impossible but Zartog could still see it after he crossed his eyes and shook his head.

'What is it?' he asked the computer.

'Like, man, that's a Tipler Cylinder,' the computer told him. 'It's going to be built next year.'

Zartog frowned. 'If it's going to be built next year, what's it doing here now?'

'Like, man, that's the Tipler thing. Soon as you build one, it's always been there.'

'That doesn't make much sense,' Zartog said.

There was a click as the computer switched circuits. 'Nothing makes, like, sense when you're dealing with a time machine.'

Fourteen

Rachel felt a little nervous as she left for school next morning. She knew the bullies would be waiting for her when school was over.

She knew that if she ran away they were big enough and fast enough to catch her.

She knew she wouldn't take them by surprise a second time.

She knew they would be out to get her big time.

All the same, she wasn't as nervous as she'd thought she'd be. She'd packed the remote control into her schoolbag.

By now she knew exactly what the control could do.

If you pointed it at something and

pressed POWER OFF, the something disappeared. The ON button brought it back again.

If you pressed the CHANNEL-CHANGE button, things changed into other things in a sequence that eventually brought them back to themselves.

There was a green button that made things grow bigger and an orange button that made them smaller again.

She also knew this was not the remote control Lord Percy had taken out into the

wood. It was something dropped from
the flying saucer.

Rachel thought about the remote
control a lot as she did her lessons. At one
point she thought about it so much her
teacher told her she was wool-gathering.

She switched it from her schoolbag to
her pocket as she left the school that
afternoon.

As she expected, Sammy Tucks, Tom
Barlow and Elvis Fine were waiting for
her at the corner.

Fifteen

'Like, wheee!' said the computer.

The saucer shivered slightly, then headed like an arrow towards the Tipler Cylinder.

'Hold on a minute!' Zartog said, but didn't have the right remote, so the computer ignored him.

They seemed to be flying directly towards the violet coloured ring.

'What's happening?' Zartog asked. 'What's happening? What's happening?'

When he asked a question three times, computers were compelled to answer.

'Like, the cylinder's so big it twists time, man!' the computer exclaimed.

The violet coloured ring grew larger.

'The red ring is the null time zone

where time stands still,' the computer said excitedly.

The violet ring grew larger still.

'The white ring is the forwards time zone where you fly into the future,' the computer told him.

The violet ring grew enormous.

'The black ring is the backwards time zone where you, like, fly into the past.'

The violet ring was now so large and so

close it filled the whole of the horizon.

'What's the violet ring?' asked Zartog anxiously.

'That's, like, the deadly zone,' the computer told him cheerfully. 'Man, you don't want to know what happens to you there.'

Zartog swallowed.

Zartog whispered, 'Heeeeelp!'

The saucer swerved and plunged into the heart of the impossibly glowing black ring.

Sixteen

'You won't get away this time,' Elvis Fine told Rachel menacingly as he walked towards her. She was pleased to notice he was still limping.

Rachel looked around. There was no one else in sight. 'You'd better leave me alone,' she told him. She had a feeling he wasn't going to pay much attention.

Elvis Fine paid no attention. 'You kicked me, Frizzhead. Do you remember that?'

Rachel said nothing. The other two hadn't moved from the corner so there was a small gap between them and Elvis Fine. She tried to figure what would happen if she darted between them.

'My knee's all swole,' growled Elvis

Fine. 'It's all swole up and red and that's your fault.'

Rachel wondered if she should point out he was the one who'd started it. She wondered if she should tell him it was his behaviour made her kick him in the knee.

She thought about this for a while then decided he wouldn't like being told that.

So she started to wonder something else instead.

She started to wonder if she really could get away with darting between them.

If his knee really was all swole up and red, he mightn't be able to run as fast as usual.

Rachel darted between Elvis Fine and his two friends.

'Frizzhead's running!' called out Sammy Tucks.

'Frizzhead's getting away!' called out Tom Barlow.

They were both grinning broadly. They

stepped out from the corner to block off her escape.

Rachel didn't even try to run past them. Instead she swung round, doubled back and raced in a wide arc round Elvis Fine. With his limp and his knee she knew he'd never catch her.

But Elvis Fine did catch her. He moved just as fast as ever and in four long strides he'd grabbed her by the arm. There was no sign of his limp, no hint of a painful knee.

'She fell for it!' squealed Sammy Tucks delightedly.

Rachel wriggled and struggled, but he held her fast. 'Leave me alone!' she wailed. 'Why can't you leave me alone?'

'Leave you alone?' echoed Elvis Fine. 'Frizzhead, you won't believe what we're going to do to you!' He raised his free hand as if to hit her.

Rachel pulled the remote from her pocket.

'You're going to wish you were never born,' he told her with that nasty grin of his. He closed his raised hand into a fist.

Rachel pointed the remote at him and pushed the POWER OFF button.

Elvis Fine disappeared.

Seventeen

Zartog stared through the window of his flying saucer. Below him was the huge blue and white ball of an alien planet, the third one from a yellow alien sun.

It was absolutely forbidden to land on an alien planet if you were Zartog's age.

Zartog frowned.

It was forbidden by the Grand Council for Forbidden Things.

It was forbidden by the Popess of Religion.

It was forbidden by the Leader of the Purple Clans.

It was forbidden by all three of Zartog's parents.

Zartog pointed the remote. 'Land saucer,' he instructed.

'Like, wow, heavy!' muttered the computer slyly.

Zartog had the most peculiar feeling he'd been here before.

The saucer plunged into the atmosphere of the alien planet. At once it started to glow.

Radar stations across the globe picked up the trace, but the operators ignored it because they didn't believe in flying saucers.

The saucer flew over Beijing, but the Chinese just thought somebody was juggling plates.

The saucer flew over New York, but the New Yorkers shrugged it off as a publicity stunt.

Zartog frowned again. New York seemed terribly familiar.

The saucer flew over Dublin, but the Irish put it down to Guinness.

Easter Island missed it altogether because the saucer flew across at Pentecost.

Zartog's frown deepened. Easter Island seemed familiar too.

The saucer flew over London. Nobody noticed because it was four o'clock and they were having tea.

Eventually the saucer hovered over a clearing in a wood located on a farm outside a small town in the Home Counties.

'Like, wow, a suitable landing space has

been found,' the computer reported, watching Zartog carefully.

Zartog stared at the computer thoughtfully. The feeling he'd been here before had grown very, very strong.

All the same, he unfastened his seat belt and slipped the remote into his pocket. He sang the note that opened the saucer door and caused a glittering silver ramp to slide out onto the ground.

'Forbidden to breathe alien air,' the computer warned. 'Forbidden to touch alien soil.'

'Like, wow, scary!' Zartog said. He started to walk down the ramp.

'Like, stop,' said the computer.

Zartog stopped.

'Look outside, man,' the computer told him.

Zartog looked outside and found they'd landed in the middle of a group of great, tall, slow life forms.

'Don't you remember?' asked the computer.

Zartog frowned one more time. The great slow life forms reminded him of his uncle, but apart from that . . .

'Hey, man,' urged the computer, 'don't you remember we've been here before?

Don't you remember this is where you lost your remote?'

Suddenly it all came back.

Zartog remembered the big life form

that looked a bit like him in an ugly alien sort of way.

He remembered the little life form full of fierceness, growls and teeth. He remembered the hopping life form that mistook him for a lettuce.

Most of all, he remembered losing his remote!

'See, man,' the computer told him smugly, 'I've brought you back in time so you don't have to do any of the stuff you did.

'You don't have to chase the rabbit.

'You don't have to drop your remote.

'You don't have to pick up the wrong one and get stuck out here with no way home.

'You don't even have to leave the saucer. I've saved you, man! I've saved you!'

Zartog said, 'I think I'll just take the smallest, tiny little look outside.'

Eighteen

'Where's Elvis gone?' asked Sammy Tucks in sudden alarm.

'I don't know,' said Tom Barlow.

They looked around. The street was empty, except for Rachel and themselves.

There was a torn page from somebody's school-book blowing on the pavement.

Sammy Tucks looked underneath it as if Elvis might be hiding there.

'He was here a minute ago,' Tom Barlow said.

'He was right here with us,' Sammy Tucks confirmed.

Sammy looked up the street while Tom looked down the street. All either of them saw was nothing.

'Perhaps he ran away,' suggested Rachel. 'Perhaps you should go and look for him.'

'Elvis wouldn't run away from any smelly little frizzhead,' sneered Sammy Tucks.

'Elvis wouldn't run away from you,' Tom Barlow scowled.

But for all the sneers and scowls, they both looked just a little frightened.

'Where is he then?' asked Rachel reasonably.

She hoped that disappearing Elvis Fine would be enough to make the others go away.

She didn't want to use her remote any more than she had to.

She thought the battery might run down.

'I expect he's . . .' Sammy Tucks waved his head about and looked up at the sky, '. . . gone for a walk!'

Tom Barlow pointed his nose skywards

too. 'I expect he's been called away on business!'

They looked down at the pavement. They looked at one another. Then they glared at Rachel. 'What have you done with him?' they demanded together.

Rachel looked back at them innocently.

She tried to hide the remote behind her back. Then she tried to slip it into her pocket.

'What's that in your hand?' snapped
Sammy Tucks. He made to grab the
remote.

Rachel pushed the CHANNEL-
CHANGE and turned him into a
hamster.

Nineteen

It was really neat for Zartog knowing what would happen.

He looked at the great slow life forms and heard himself say, 'Take me to your leader.'

He walked about a bit and sensed the familiar life forms in the neighbourhood.

He watched out for the hopping life form with big ears and levitated three feet off the ground as it approached him.

The hopping life form jumped and leaped but couldn't reach his toes to nibble them.

After a while it got bored with the game and hopped off to find a more convenient lettuce.

Zartog felt his pocket. The remote control was still there.

He floated back to earth and looked round for the wrong remote. He found it lying in the middle of the clearing.

As he bent to pick it up, his own remote fell from his pocket onto the ground.

Zartog smiled and picked it up again. His teachers told him once that changing time was tricky, but this was easy-peasy.

Now he had two remotes, the wrong one and the right one. The wrong one looked like something chewed it and had made in Hong Kong stamped on the bottom, just like he remembered.

Zartog stashed away the wrong remote in his zip-up purse. He slipped the right remote safely back into his pocket.

Then he waited for the next life forms to appear.

He knew they would both look extremely scary, but now he had his proper remote, he could change them into something harmless.

He could change them into grindleworms and watch them wiggle.

He could change them into Borian light bulbs.

He could change them into fones or wans or scrumblegrunts. He could change them into hects or lects or limians. He could change them into pordles that leaped over hurdles, grogs not much bigger than hogs, lishes as harmless as dishes. He could –

The two large, fast life forms appeared. Zartog remembered them well. The one with the huge glare lenses looked even more scary second time around.

But Zartog felt no fear. He drew the remote – the right remote – out of his pocket and pointed it towards them.

'Woof!'

The smaller life form hurled itself towards him, snatched the remote from his hand and raced off with it in its mouth.

'Yipes!' wailed Zartog and ran back to his flying saucer.

Twenty

Rachel shivered suddenly as if a goose had walked over her grave. She had the strangest feeling something had changed, but couldn't imagine what.

She was still holding the magic remote she'd rescued from Lord Percy after he'd snatched it from the flying saucer person.

Elvis Fine was still safely disappeared and Sammy Tucks remained a hamster.

It crouched on the pavement near her feet, twitching its nose nervously.

Tom Barlow looked at Rachel in disbelief. Then he looked at the hamster in disbelief. Then he looked back at Rachel. 'You did that!' he shouted. He ran towards her, fists raised.

Rachel pushed the CHANNEL-
CHANGE again.

Tom Barlow turned into a mouse. The
mouse and the hamster looked at each
other, noses twitching.

Rachel turned the remote to the place
where Elvis Fine had been standing and
pressed the ON button. Elvis reappeared
at once, his face a picture of
bewilderment.

'Where am I?' he asked. 'Where's
Sammy? Where's Tom?'

'Right beside you, Elvis!' Rachel told
him. She pointed to the hamster and the
mouse.

'No jokes!' said Elvis Fine sternly and
took a step towards her.

Rachel turned him into the sweetest
little bunny rabbit you ever saw.

Then she turned the rabbit into a mole,
the mouse into a weasel and the hamster
into a kitten.

She turned the kitten into a pup, the

mouse into a snake and the mole into a
penguin.

She turned the penguin into a worm,
the snake into a hedgehog and the puppy
into a pair of glasses.

She turned the pair of glasses into fox,
the hedgehog into a duck and the worm
into a pony.

The fox began to chase the duck, so she
changed them both into cooing doves.

She changed the pony into a sheep for good measure.

Then she changed one dove into a cow and the other into a camel.

She changed the sheep into a goat and the goat into a crow and the camel into a rainbow-bottomed baboon, the cow into a cat, the cat into a dog, the crow into a ferret, the baboon into an owl, the dog into a bat, the ferret into a pack of cards, the owl into a spider, the spider into a frog, the cards into a fly and the bat into a fish that flapped on the grass.

She turned the fish into a stoat, the fly into a hawk, the frog into a kangaroo, the stoat into a wildebeest, the hawk into a donkey, the 'roo into a beetle, the beetle into a bottle, the donkey into a sloth, the wildebeest into a mongoose.

Then she changed the mongoose into Tom Barlow, the sloth into Elvis Fine and the bottle into Sammy Tucks.

They took one look at her and ran.

Twenty-One

'Man, that was really dumb,' said the computer with an electronic sigh.

'I didn't chase the rabbit this time,' Zartog told it sheepishly.

'No, man, but you still managed to, like, lose your remote.'

Zartog stared gloomily through the saucer window. They were back in orbit round the lovely blue-white planet exactly as they'd been before.

The only remote he had was the stupid made in Hong Kong chewed-up useless old thing he'd had before.

The computer wouldn't take him home to Sirius, just like it wouldn't take him home before.

Without the right remote he was stuck

orbiting this rotten planet for ever.

And there was no way he could get the
right remote back from those scary alien
life forms down below.

In fact, there was absolutely nothing he
could do.

Unless he went back in time again and
tried again, again.

'How about we go back to the Tipler
Cylinder?' he said to the computer.

'No can do,' the computer said. 'First

time's free, but after that they charge
you.'

'How much?' asked Zartog quickly.

'Like, more than we got with us,' the
computer told him gloomily.

Acid tears began to form in the corners
of Zartog's huge, nocturnal eyes.

'So we can't go home?'

'Not without the right remote, man.'

'I'll never see my parents again?'

'Looks that way.'

'And we can't go back in time a second time?'

''Fraid not.'

'So I'm doomed to stay in orbit round this rotten planet for ever and ever and ever?' The tears were flowing freely now, etching little channels in the metal of the floor.

'Yeah, right,' the computer said. 'Man can't do nothing when he don't have the right remote.'

'But how do I get the right remote?' howled Zartog, not for the first time in his short, eventful life.

The computer brightened up at once. 'Like, wow,' it said, 'I thought you'd never ask!'

Twenty-Two

That night, Rachel woke up to find a bright light shining through her window. She climbed out of bed.

Somehow she wasn't surprised to see the flying saucer that had landed in the meadow just beyond the house.

She pulled on her dressing gown and a pair of wellington boots, then dug out the remote control she'd hidden in her socks drawer.

She dropped it into the dressing gown pocket.

'Woof!' said Lord Percy softly as she crept into the kitchen.

'No, I'm fine,' she whispercd. 'But the flying saucer has come back.'

'Woof.'

'I thought I'd better,' Rachel said. She suspected the little alien was looking for his remote. While she'd have liked to keep it, she knew that would be stealing.

Besides, she didn't think the bullies would be troubling her again.

'Woof.'

'Of course you can,' said Rachel. To tell the truth she was quite pleased to have the company. Flying saucers made her nervous.

She unlatched the back door quietly

and they slipped out of the house.

A ramp emerged from the flying saucer as she approached and the little person with very large eyes walked towards her, one hand extended.

Rachel's heart lurched when she saw the hand was holding a remote control.

As she came closer, she noticed it had teeth marks in it.

Rachel stopped.

The space person stopped and twisted his left ear. 'I am Zartog,' he said

carefully in English. 'Will you help me? I can't get home unless you do.'

Lord Percy sniffed at him, then backed off, hackles rising. 'Woof!' he said fiercely. 'Woof! Woof! Woof!'

The space person twisted his left ear again. 'Woof!' he said to Lord Percy.

'Woof, woof, woof-woof, WOOF!'

Lord Percy blinked, then wagged his tail.

The space person turned back to Rachel. 'Where I come from, the penalty for losing your remote is to have your stomach sewn up so you can't eat chocolate.

'After which they cover you with glow-paint so grindlewinkles find you in the dark.

'They remove your feet so you can't walk. They nail up your mouth so you can't talk.

'They stop your allowance and keep you in detention. They give you extra

homework and make you do the
housework.

'They unscrew your belly button so
your bum keeps falling off.'

Rachel felt a sudden surge of sympathy.
She took the remote control from her
dressing gown pocket and held it out.

Zartog took it and gently handed her
the chewed control. 'Thank you,' he said
politely.

He walked back inside and withdrew

the ramp. Dimly, Rachel heard a new voice say, 'Hey, man, didn't I tell you these life forms were suckers for a good sob story?'

Rachel bristled, but Zartog only said, 'You're wrong. She's just a very honest, decent, upright, sympathetic sort of life form. I'd quite like to be like her myself.'

'Wow,' said the second voice admiringly, 'have you learned a heavy lesson!'

'Engage warp drive,' said Zartog firmly.

'Like, wow, right away,' the second voice replied.

The flying saucer disappeared.

Frowning, Rachel walked back to the house.